Who's That Knocking on Christmas Eve?

JAN BRETT

G. P. PUTNAM'S SONS ✤ NEW YORK

For
Lia

Printed in Hong Kong by South China Printing Co. (1988) Ltd. Designed by Gunta Alexander. Text set in Goudy. The art was done in watercolors and gouache. Airbrush backgrounds by Joseph Hearne.
Library of Congress Cataloging-in-Publication Data   Brett, Jan, 1949–   Who's that knocking on Christmas Eve? / Jan Brett.
p. cm.   Summary: A boy from Finnmark and his ice bear help scare away some hungry trolls so that Kyri and her father can enjoy their Christmas Eve meal. [1. Trolls—Fiction. 2. Christmas—Fiction. 3. Norway—Fiction.] I. Title. PZ7.B75225 Kn 2002
[E]—dc21 2001048253   ISBN 0-399-23873-5   10 9 8 7 6 5 4 3 2 1 First Impression

High above the Arctic Circle in the land of ice and snow,
the northern lights shimmer in the night like a curtain of color
hanging from the sky.

The air is so crisp and clear in this northern place that one Christmas Eve long ago, a boy from Finnmark, on his way to Oslo with his ice bear, could see smoke curling up from a hut far in the distance. He was cold and hungry, so he headed toward it.

Far off in another direction, someone else smelled the smoke, and even though he couldn't see it, he raced off to tell the others.

As the boy from Finnmark made his way toward the hut, Kyri was
inside feeding the fire that made the smoke that roasted and baked
the fine food.

Delicious sausage and fish and tasty buns and cakes were all laid out

on a pine table. Sweet porridge bubbled over the fire, and apple cider stayed cool on the windowsill.

So why did Kyri jump at every creak in the sod roof? And why did she run to the window when an icicle fell into the snow?

It was because in years past on Christmas Eve, trolls came when they smelled the delicious aromas coming from the hut. They would pound on the door until it burst open, and they wouldn't leave until they had eaten up every bit of the Christmas Eve meal.

"No troll invasion this year," Kyri's father had said. "I'm going up the mountain to watch and chase them away." And off he had gone to stop the trouble before it began.

So this year, Kyri was alone in the hut when she heard a soft
sound at the door.

Knockety knock, knockety knock.

Someone was out there, but surely it was too polite a knock
for it to be a troll.

Kyri went to the door and peeked out.

There was the boy from Finnmark with his ice bear.

"Please let me inside to warm up," he said. "I am on my way south to show off my bear for the townsfolk of Oslo. I've many frosty miles behind me, and many more to go."

"Come in," Kyri said, "but I have to warn you that, in years past, our house has been invaded by a pack of hungry trolls."

"Trolls would be a welcome adventure," the boy said.

So he came in, and the ice bear crawled under the warm stove and fell asleep.

Kyri and the boy had just settled down in front of the
fire when they heard, not so softly this time,

Knockety knock, knockety knock!

"There's no one home," the boy called out. He was
certain it was trolls, so he pushed the big chest in front
of the door.

When all was quiet, Kyri and the boy sat down in front of the fire again.
Kyri got to thinking. *I wonder if the porridge is creamy enough.* And she ladled
a bit of it into bowls for each of them.

They had just raised their bowls when they heard a loud . . .

Knockety knock, knockety knock!

It was as if someone was pounding on the door with a big rock.

"No one at home!" the boy from Finnmark shouted, and he ran to lock all the windows.

It was quiet again, but the delicious smells wafted around the hut. Kyri got to thinking. *Is the sausage salty enough?* She took a piece for herself and gave one to the boy. They had just raised their forks when they heard a thunderous . . .

Knockety knock, knockety knock!

The hut shook, and they heard a loud *crack*. It was the cellar trapdoor
splintering open.

Kyri and the boy ran into the animal shed and pulled the door shut
just as a torrent of noisy trolls burst up from the cellar.

There were bat-eared trolls, there were bug-nosed trolls, and
each troll was wilder and more raucous than the one before!
They munched and grunted, shrieked and cackled, splashed
the cider, and crammed themselves with Christmas cakes.

Then, when they were through stuffing themselves, they
tumbled about, pinching each other, stamping on one another's
toes, and tweaking their long snouts, which is how trolls have
a good time.

But through the ruckus and din, the littlest troll spied the ice bear under the stove.

He took the hot morsel of sausage he had been roasting in the fire and screeched, "Have a bit of sausage, Kitty!" And he poked the sleeping bear's nose with it.

The ice bear leaped up with a tremendous roar, his nose
burning terribly. Growling, he chased the little troll and all the
big trolls around the table, up the walls, and out the windows.

"Scratch them, Kitty!"

Kyri and the boy cheered as they watched the trolls
scramble off through the ice and snow, howling.

Up on the hill, Kyri's father heard the shouts, so he
raced down on his skis.

When he saw the trolls, Kyri's father could tell in an instant that
they wanted to be as far away from the little hut as they could be.
"Good-bye, trolls," he shouted as they disappeared up the
mountain, and he skied home.

"What a fine bear you have!" he told the boy from Finnmark.
"Thank you for scaring away those pesky trolls. You must come back
next year for a real Christmas Eve feast on your way home from Oslo."
And they all sat down for some porridge.

A year later, Kyri was on the mountain, gathering
wood to make the fire to cook their dinner for Christmas Eve,
when the littlest troll popped out from behind a snowbank.

"Missy," he called in a high, crackly voice, "do you still have
that kitty that sleeps under the stove?"

"Oh, yes," Kyri said, "only she has grown up into a big cat now,
and she has seven kittens, all larger and fiercer than herself."

"Awk," he screeched, "then we won't be visiting *your* hut on Christmas Eve." And he disappeared into a huge snowdrift.